BILLY
AND THE
REBEL

BASED ON A TRUE CIVIL WAR STORY

BY DEBORAH HOPKINSON
ILLUSTRATED BY BRIAN FLOCA

ALADDIN PAPERBACKS
NEW YORK LONDON TORONTO SYDNEY

To the Ruzicka family:
Marvin, Cheri, Alex, and Michelle
—D. H.

For Greg Street
—B. F.

ALADDIN PAPERBACKS
An imprint of Simon & Schuster Children's Publishing Division
1230 Avenue of the Americas, New York, NY 10020
Text copyright © 2005 by Deborah Hopkinson
Illustrations copyright © 2005 by Brian Floca
All rights reserved, including the right of reproduction in whole or in part in any form.
READY-TO-READ is a registered trademark of Simon & Schuster, Inc.
ALADDIN PAPERBACKS and colophon are trademarks of Simon & Schuster, Inc.
Also available in an Atheneum Books for Young Readers hardcover edition.
Designed by Abelardo Martínez
The text of this book was set in Century Old Style.
The illustrations were rendered in watercolors.
Manufactured in the United States of America
First Aladdin Paperbacks edition March 2006
10 9 8
The Library of Congress has cataloged the hardcover edition as follows:
Hopkinson, Deborah.
Billy and the rebel / by Deborah Hopkinson ; illustrated by Brian Floca.
p. cm—(Ready-to-Read)
Summary: During the Battle of Gettysburg in 1863, a mother and son shelter a young Confederate deserter. Includes a historical note on the incident.
ISBN-13: 978-0-689-83964-1 (hc.)
ISBN-10: 0-689-83964-2 (hc.)
1. Gettysburg (Pa.), Battle of, 1863—Juvenile fiction. 2. United States—History—Civil War, 1861–1865—Desertions—Juvenile fiction. [1. Gettysburg (Pa.), Battle of, 1863—Fiction. 2. United States—History—Civil War, 1861–1865—Desertions—Fiction. 3. Soldiers—Fiction.] I. Floca, Brian, ill. II. Title. III. Series.
PZ7.H778125 Bg 2002
[Fic]—dc21
2001022982
ISBN-13: 978-0-689-83396-0 (Aladdin pbk.)
ISBN-10: 0-689-83396-2 (Aladdin pbk.)
0518 LAK

Contents:

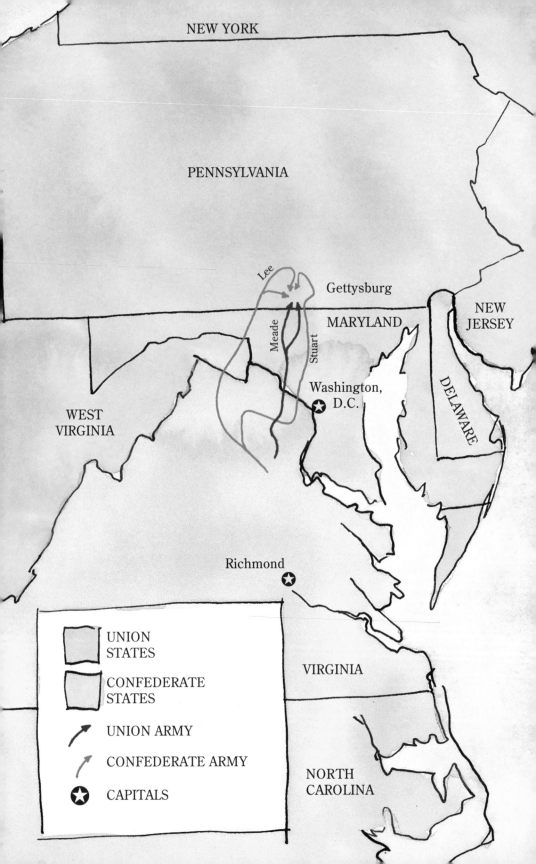

NEW YORK

PENNSYLVANIA

Lee

Gettysburg

MARYLAND

NEW JERSEY

Meade

Stuart

Washington, D.C.

DELAWARE

WEST VIRGINIA

Richmond

UNION STATES

CONFEDERATE STATES

UNION ARMY

CONFEDERATE ARMY

CAPITALS

VIRGINIA

NORTH CAROLINA

Chapter One
The Battle Begins

One hot July day Billy climbed the hill
near his house to look for raspberries.
Just as he plopped a juicy berry into his
mouth, Billy heard the sound of a musket.
Crack! He looked into the valley below.

Billy forgot all about the raspberries. His heart began to beat as loud as that gun. Billy turned and ran home so fast he made a cloud of dust on the dirt road.

"Mama, I saw soldiers!" he cried.

Mama frowned. "How many soldiers, Billy?"

"Too many to count," said Billy.

"What will happen, Mama?"

"I'm afraid there will be a battle," she said.

Billy knew the war had been going on for two years. Union soldiers from the North were fighting with Rebel soldiers from the South. Papa said there were many reasons for the war. The North and the South had grown far apart. They did not agree about important things.

There had been many battles already. Now the Confederate Army was invading the North. Rebel soldiers were right in Gettysburg!

Suddenly Billy remembered that Papa had gone into town that morning.

"What will Papa do now, Mama?" he asked.

"I'm sure he'll stay in town and hide in your uncle's house until the battle is over," Mama said.

Billy hugged his mother tightly. "I hope Papa will be safe," he whispered.

Chapter Two
Soldiers on the Farm

Boom! Boom! Billy heard cannons.
The battle had started. Billy wished he
could hide under the hay until it was over,
but Mama needed him. Their farm was
near the camp of some Rebel soldiers.

Soon Billy saw soldiers coming
into his yard. The soldiers were hungry.
They wanted food. The soldiers killed
their chickens, one by one.

"Cook these chickens," they told
Mama.

Mama did as the soldiers asked.

When it was dark, the Rebel soldiers went back to their camp. But the next day was the same. Billy heard more guns. More hungry soldiers came to the farm.

"Will Papa come home today?" Billy asked Mama.

"No," said Mama. "The battle isn't over yet."

Chapter Three
A Midnight Knock

That night Billy lay awake. The loud
guns were quiet. Billy could hear the
sounds of a soft July night. He heard an
owl hoot. He heard crickets singing in
the grass. Then Billy heard a new sound.

Knock! Knock!

"Papa!" cried Billy.

Billy and his mother ran downstairs.
The wooden steps creaked in the still
house. Billy's mother held a candle.

"Who's there?" she called.

Billy heard a soft voice call, "Please, let me in."

They unlocked the door. It wasn't Papa at all! Instead it was a boy. In the candlelight, Billy could see that he wore a dirty, gray uniform. This boy was a Confederate soldier.

"Ma'am, I ran away from camp," the stranger said. "I can't go on. I'm scared." Billy saw that the soldier was trembling.

Mama said, "Why, you're just a boy. You're too young to be in this war. Stay here. We'll keep you safe."

"Where are you from?" asked Billy.

"North Carolina," said the Rebel. "But I dare not tell you my name."

"Then we will call you Cousin," said Billy.

The boy was hungry, so Billy's mother gave him some milk and bread. He was tired, so Billy took him to the attic.

"You can sleep here," said Billy. "Hide under the quilts like a cat and no one will find you."

Chapter Four
Billy Guards the Farm

The next morning Mama woke Billy early.

"I must leave you for a while," she said softly. "Many Union soldiers have been hurt. I must bring them water and bandages."

Billy reached up and hugged Mama.
Then he helped Mama saddle their
old horse. Billy and Mama loaded food,
water, and bandages into a basket.

"Be careful today, Billy," said Mama.

"Don't worry about me, Mama," said
Billy. "The soldiers need you more. I'll take
good care of the farm."

"Give Cousin some of your clothes,"
Mama told Billy. "And if any Rebels
come, don't let Cousin talk to them."

"Why not?" Billy asked.

"Cousin sounds like someone from
the South," said Mama. "If they hear him,
they might guess that he has run away.
And who knows how they might punish
him."

Billy nodded. "I won't let him talk
to any soldiers."

Chapter Five
Billy's Warning

Billy gave Cousin a shirt and pants. He cooked the last chicken egg and gave it to Cousin for breakfast.

All at once the roar of a cannon shook the house. Guns cracked like thunder,

and smoke from the battle filled the sky.
Billy and Cousin listened and watched
together.

"I'm glad you're here," Billy said
to Cousin.

Soon more Rebel soldiers arrived at Billy's farm.

"We're starving. Cook us some chickens," they said.

"You have killed all our chickens," said Billy.

"Then give us some bread," they ordered.

"We have no bread left," said Billy.

"What can you give us, then?" asked a soldier.

Billy didn't want to give the soldiers anything.

But at last he said, "Well, the cherries on our trees are ripe. I suppose we can give you cherries."

Billy and Cousin climbed the cherry trees. They cut down branches full of red, sweet fruit. They gave ripe cherries to the hungry soldiers.

As he sat in the tree, Billy began to worry. He worried about Papa, hiding in town. He worried about Mama, helping the Union soldiers. And he worried about Cousin, feeding cherries to the Rebels.

"Be careful," Billy whispered to him. "Don't talk to any of these soldiers. They might guess that you are one of them."

Chapter Six
Cousin Takes a Chance

At the end of the day the guns stopped.
A Rebel soldier rode into the yard.

He said, "We must go. The battle
has ended and the North has won."

Billy was glad to see the soldiers go.

"Listen," he said to Cousin. "Everything is quiet. That soldier was right. The battle is over. My mama and papa should be home soon."

Cousin said, "Let's go to the road to watch for them."

The smoke was so thick Billy could barely see the yellow sun sink behind the hills. The road was crowded with Rebel soldiers leaving Gettysburg.

They were covered with dirt and dust. Many had bandages on their arms and legs. The soldiers hung their heads and dragged their feet. They had lost the battle.

One soldier on a horse rode close to Billy.

"Get out of my way, Yankee!" he shouted.

The Rebel's horse reared up at Billy. Billy had been mad and scared for three days. Suddenly all his feelings burst out. He wanted to throw the soldier from his horse.

"Watch it, mister!" yelled Billy. "Get out of here and go back to where you belong!"

The man glared at Billy. He had been mad and scared too. He began to shout at Billy. He even put his hand near his gun.

In a flash Cousin stepped in front of
Billy. He pushed his hat out to the soldier
and smiled.

"Don't mind my friend, sir," he said.
"Look, I have some sweet cherries here
in my hat. Wouldn't you like to have some?"

When the soldier saw the cherries, he forgot about Billy. He grabbed Cousin's hat, kicked his horse, and rode off down the road.

Chapter Seven
Billy and Cousin

Billy looked at Cousin.

"You shouldn't have spoken to that soldier," Billy said. "If he'd found out you were a Rebel, he might have taken you away."

"I wanted to help you," Cousin said.

Billy put out his hand to Cousin.
"Thank you. You're very brave."

Cousin shook Billy's hand and
laughed.

"I was not a very brave soldier," he
said. "But maybe I can be a brave friend."

Just then Mama came riding toward them.

"Mama!" cried Billy. "Are you all right?"

Mama climbed down from her horse. She wiped the dust from her face with her apron.

"I've seen a terrible battle today," she said. "It's good to come home and find a boy from the South and a boy from the North laughing together. I hope this war will be over soon and that we can all live together in peace."

Billy heard someone call his name.
Billy threw himself into his father's arms.

"Papa!" he cried. "I was so worried."

Papa lifted Billy off the ground in a big bear hug.

"I came as soon as it was safe, Billy." Then Papa saw Cousin.

"But who is this?" he asked.

Billy put his hand on Cousin's shoulder and smiled. "This is my friend."

Author's Note

Billy and the Rebel was inspired by a true story that took place during the Battle of Gettysburg, July 1-3, 1863. This three-day battle was one of the worst of the Civil War, and it changed that sleepy town forever. Afterward, many people who lived near Gettysburg wrote about their experiences. Two of them were William Bayly and his mother, Harriet Hamilton Bayly.

The real Billy Bayly was thirteen in 1863. The Bayly farm was near a Rebel camp, and many Rebel